♥ Mindy Kim and the
Lunar New Year Parade ♥

**Don't miss more fun adventures
with Mindy Kim!**

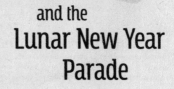

Mindy Kim

and the
Lunar New Year Parade

BOOK
2

By Lyla Lee
Illustrated by Dung Ho

ALADDIN
New York London Toronto Sydney New Delhi

This book is a work of fiction. Any references to historical events, real people, or real places are used fictitiously. Other names, characters, places, and events are products of the author's imagination, and any resemblance to actual events or places or persons, living or dead, is entirely coincidental.

ALADDIN

An imprint of Simon & Schuster Children's Publishing Division

1230 Avenue of the Americas, New York, New York 10020

First Aladdin paperback edition January 2020

Text copyright © 2020 by Lyla Lee

Illustrations copyright © 2020 by Dung Ho

Also available in an Aladdin hardcover edition.

All rights reserved, including the right of reproduction in whole or in part in any form.

ALADDIN and related logo are registered trademarks of Simon & Schuster, Inc.

For information about special discounts for bulk purchases, please contact Simon & Schuster Special Sales at 1-866-506-1949 or business@simonandschuster.com.

The Simon & Schuster Speakers Bureau can bring authors to your live event. For more information or to book an event contact the Simon & Schuster Speakers Bureau at 1-866-248-3049 or visit our website at www.simonspeakers.com.

Book designed by Laura Lyn DiSiena

The illustrations for this book were rendered digitally.

The text of this book was set in Haboro.

Manufactured in the United States of America 1219 OFF

10 9 8 7 6 5 4 3 2 1

Library of Congress Control Number 2019948664

ISBN 978-1-5344-4011-1 (hc)

ISBN 978-1-5344-4010-4 (pbk)

ISBN 978-1-5344-4012-8 (eBook)

To my parents, who always kept me connected
to my Korean culture

Mindy Kim and the
Lunar New Year Parade

Chapter 1

My name is Mindy Kim.

I'm almost eight years old, or at least, that's how old I am in the United States. In Korea, though, I'm nine! That's what Dad told me as he drove me to school.

"Korean people calculate age differently," he said. "You're already one year old when you're born, and then you get one year older on New Year's Day, instead of getting older on your birthday."

I got really excited, since it's been eight years since I was born. One plus eight is nine, and nine years old was *definitely* old enough to get a puppy.

And even better yet, Lunar New Year was this Saturday!

"Does this mean that I'll turn ten this weekend?" I asked, throwing my backpack in the back seat.

Dad laughed. "No, silly. People only age up on the first of January *or* on Lunar New Year, not both."

I sat back into my seat with a big huff. "What's

the point of two New Years if you can only age up on one?"

Dad shook his head as he pulled into the school's parking lot. "It's an important part of our culture, Mindy. It goes way back to the times when our ancestors in Korea used the lunar calendar to tell time. Tell you what, why don't we go to the Lunar New Year parade in Orlando this weekend? I saw an ad for it the other day. It looks like it'll be fun!"

Dad smiled at me, but I was unconvinced. The last time Dad said something would be "fun," I ended up watching a boring show about really slow slugs all by myself because he fell asleep in five minutes.

Plus, so much has changed since the last time we celebrated Lunar New Year. Last year, Dad, Mom, and I celebrated with the other Korean people in our neighborhood. We played really fun games like yutnori and jegichagi, ate so many yummy rice cakes, and even sang karaoke! There was no way that we could have as much fun this year as we did then.

Not without Mom.

Now the only other Korean family in our neighborhood is Eunice's, and they were going to Seattle to visit their relatives for the holiday. It was just going to be me and Dad.

"The parade will be fun," Dad said again. "It'll be good for us to leave the house."

I sighed. Dad really wanted to go to the parade! And I didn't want to make him sad by saying I didn't want to go.

"Okay," I said. "I'll go to the parade."

Dad beamed. "Great! See you after school, honey."

"Bye, Appa," I said, using the Korean word for "Daddy."

I headed toward the school, my shoulders slumped. I was not looking forward to Lunar New Year. Not anymore.

Chapter 2

After school was over, Eunice picked me up like usual. But since Dad was working super late today, she took us to her house instead of going to mine.

"So, Mindy, are you excited for Lunar New Year?" Eunice asked while we were doing homework in her room.

"Not really," I said. "We're not really doing anything. Just going to a parade in Orlando."

"Ooh, parades are fun, though! I heard the Orlando one is really good. It got so popular that they had to move it to a larger location to fit all the people!"

"I wish we were going on vacation, like you," I said. "It's gonna be really lonely with just Dad and me. Even with all the people at the parade."

Eunice stopped writing in her notebook for a second. And then her face lit up with a smile.

"Hold on, I have an idea. Why don't you take a break from homework to play with Oliver? I'll be right back."

I shrugged. "Okay."

After Eunice left, I looked underneath the desk, where Oliver the Maltese was sleeping. He was making cute little huffy-puffy sounds. I guess that's how dogs sound when they're snoring.

"Hey, Oliver," I said softly. "Do you want to play?"

Oliver's ears twitched, but he just kept snoring away.

I sighed. That was probably a no.

Instead I went back to my homework. We were doing long division, and it was pretty easy, although sometimes the teacher threw in things called remainders, to be tricky.

"I'll get you, remainders!" I muttered to myself

as I scribbled down my answers. Soon my paper was full of numbers.

Eunice finally came back into her room, and when she did, she was grinning from ear to ear.

"Come down to the kitchen, Mindy!" she said. "I have a surprise for you."

"A surprise?" I clapped with excitement. I love surprises!

Eunice's mom greeted us both with a big hug when we came into the kitchen.

"Mindy! You came just in time! I just finished making tteokguk."

"Tteokguk!" I exclaimed. "Really? But it isn't Lunar New Year yet!"

Tteokguk is a special soup with cute, oval-shaped pieces of rice cake that everyone in Korea eats during Lunar New Year. Mom used to make it every year, because eating the rice-cake soup is supposed to give you a fresh, clean start for the new year ahead.

I was wondering if I'd get to eat tteokguk this year, but I hadn't mentioned it to Dad. I didn't want to make him sad by reminding him of Mom.

"Eunice told me that you and your dad are going to stay in Florida for the holiday," said Mrs. Park. "So I wanted to give you a little taste of home. I'll pack some leftover soup for your dad so he can eat some when he gets off work too."

Eunice's mom is so nice! I gave her a big hug and sat down at the dining room table.

The soup was nice and hot, with strips of egg, beef, and dried seaweed arranged prettily in the bowl. It was so good! Almost as good as Mom's.

To make things even better, Oliver the Maltese came to sit next to me at the dining room table. The food smells must have woken him up! He stared at me with big puppy eyes, pretty much asking me to feed him.

I snuck him a few pieces of beef. He's lucky he's cute.

When we were done eating, Mrs. Park brought us plates full of cute, colorful rice cakes.

"Both Eunice and her dad really like rice cakes, so we always end up buying too many. Why don't

you take some to share with your classmates tomorrow? It's not like we can finish them all before we go to Seattle."

I thought back to the seaweed business I started several months ago. I guess sharing was okay as long as I didn't ask for anything back. My teacher, Mrs. Potts, said only trading snacks was banned, not just giving them!

"Okay, thank you!" I said with a big bow. Dad always said that I should bow to Korean adults in two different scenarios: one, if I was seeing them for the first time that day, and two, if they did something really nice for me.

Mrs. Park smiled. "No problem. Hope you and your dad enjoy the food."

I was feeling a bit better about Lunar New Year. Yummy food always makes everything better.

Chapter 3

Every Friday, my class does "What's New with You?" show-and-tell, where people who have exciting things going on can share with the class. When it was my turn, I showed everyone the plastic container of rice cakes that Mrs. Park had packed for me to bring to school.

My teacher, Mrs. Potts, frowned. "Mindy? What are those?"

"They're rice cakes!" I explained. "Tomorrow is Lunar New Year, so I wanted to share them with the class."

Priscilla, the girl who always sits in the front of class and asks everyone questions, raised her hand.

"Yes, Priscilla?" said Mrs. Potts, giving her a small nod.

"What is Lunar New Year?"

"That's a very good question." Mrs. Potts smiled at me. "Mindy, would you like to explain to the class about Lunar New Year?"

Oh boy. I tried to remember everything I'd learned about Lunar New Year in Korean school back in California.

"A long time ago in Asia, people used the moon to tell time instead of the sun. There's a whole separate calendar based on it," I began. "Some people still use the lunar calendar, and the New Year on that calendar is called Lunar New Year. People from all over Asia celebrate it! In China, Vietnam, and Korea, too! So Lunar New Year is New Year's Day but using the moon."

"That's so cool!" said Priscilla.

And then more hands shot up. There were so many that I couldn't possibly answer everyone's questions. I answered as many as I could before Mrs. Potts said, "All right, then. That was very educational. Thank you, Mindy. Are you going to share those rice cakes with everyone in the class?"

She gave me a look.

"Don't worry, Mrs. Potts, I'm not gonna try to trade them or anything. They're one hundred percent free!"

A few kids giggled. Operation Yummy Seaweed Business happened months ago, but people still know me as the seaweed-business girl.

Mrs. Potts laughed too. "All right, Mindy, if you say so. Would you like to go around and give everyone a rice cake?"

"Sure!"

I started walking around the class with the rice cakes and some napkins I'd brought from home. I first gave a rice cake to Mrs. Potts, because Dad says that I should always give things to adults first. It's Korean manners! She put it in her mouth and smiled.

"That's delicious, Mindy!" she said.

I gave her my biggest smile. I was so happy that Mrs. Potts liked the rice cake!

The first kid I gave a rice cake to was, of course, Sally, my best friend. She took a pink napkin from me and then used it to carefully grab one of the rice cakes.

"Thanks, Mindy!" she said.

But not everyone was that nice.

"Ew," said Melissa, one of Sally's friends. She wrinkled her nose. "Why is it so squishy? And what's in it?"

"Red bean! It's really sweet and yummy," I explained.

"Beans?" Melissa exclaimed. "Yuck! Get it away from me!"

A lot fewer people wanted to try the rice cakes after that.

But they didn't bother me much. They were missing out! It just meant there were more rice cakes for me and everyone else who actually liked them. The people who *did* like them *really* liked them and kept asking for more!

"Mindy, you have the best taste in snacks!" said Sally.

I beamed. Sally was so nice! What she said gave me an idea. I wasn't sure if it was going to work or not, but it was worth a try.

During recess, I asked Sally, "Hey, my dad and I are going to the Lunar New Year parade in Orlando tomorrow. Do you want to come with us? I heard it'll be really fun, and there's gonna be a lot of yummy snacks."

"Oh yeah!" Sally said. "I see ads about it every year. Sure! I have to ask my mom first, but I think I can go."

"Great!"

I was really excited. The parade would be much better with Sally by my side.

Lunar New Year just got a lot more fun.

Chapter 4

Dad was really happy that I asked Sally to come with us to the parade.

"That's great, Mindy!" he said as he tucked me into bed. "The more the merrier. I'm so glad that you and Sally are such good friends."

I hugged Mr. Shiba, my favorite Shiba Inu plush, close to my chest. "Do you have any friends who might want to come, Appa?" I asked.

He shrugged. "I don't really know my coworkers that well yet, and I'm not sure if they'd be interested in coming. I'm glad you were able to find someone to come with you, though!"

That made me sad. It had been several months

since we first moved to Florida, and it didn't look like Dad had any friends. I was glad that I at least had Sally.

"You should make friends with the people you work with," I said. "Bring them food! It worked for me."

Dad chuckled. "Okay, Mindy. I'll take that into consideration. Thanks for the advice."

"No problem."

After Dad went back downstairs, I pulled my blanket over my head. I'm not scared of the dark—not anymore, anyway. But sometimes it still gets really lonely. Plus, even though I was excited, I was still worried about tomorrow. What if the parade turned out to be really boring? I'd feel bad for dragging Sally along with me.

I reached down under my bed and got out Mr. Toe Beans, my soft corgi doll. I usually sleep with only one stuffed animal to show my dad that I'm all grown-up, but tonight called for *two*.

Sandwiched in between Mr. Shiba and Mr. Toe Beans, I drifted off to sleep.

That night, I dreamed that I was back in our apartment in California. Everything seemed normal, but no matter how much I looked, I couldn't find Mom or Dad! I ran outside to see if I could find them there, but I got lost in a big crowd of people.

It was a really scary dream!

"Mindy, wake up!"

When I opened my eyes, I saw Dad standing beside my bed. He was holding up Mr. Toe Beans with a concerned look on his face.

"Are you okay?" he said. "It sounded like you were having a nightmare. Mr. Toe Beans is here for a hug if you need one!"

I reached up and took Mr. Toe Beans from Dad. Usually, I didn't want Dad to see that I still liked hugging my stuffed animals, but today was a special occasion. My face still felt wet from the tears I cried during my nightmare, and even though the real Dad was right in front of me, I still felt really sad. I squeezed Mr. Toe Beans tightly.

"Thanks, Appa," I said.

"Do you want to talk about it?" Dad asked.

I shook my head. I was afraid that if I told Dad about my dream, it'd make him sad too.

"Okay, well. Why don't you go ahead and change out of your pajamas? We need to go pick up Sally soon."

Dad went back downstairs, and I sighed. Thanks to my nightmare, now I *really* didn't want to go to the parade, even with Sally coming along with us. It was a pretty bad start to the Lunar New Year.

I went to my closet and changed into my high-five T-shirt. Dad and I call it that because it's a cute periwinkle T-shirt with a golden-retriever puppy giving a tabby kitty a high five. It made me feel a bit better.

When I sat down at the dining room table to eat my toast and cereal, I asked, "Appa, what's the zodiac animal for this new year?

My favorite thing about the lunar calendar is the fact that every year has its own special animal from the Chinese zodiac. Last year's was a cute pig. But I didn't know what came after that.

Dad thought for a moment before replying, "Hmm, it's 2020, so it's the Year of the Rat!"

"Aw," I said. "Rats are so cute!"

I thought about Mr. Ratowski, the classroom pet rat that my old teacher had back in California. He was really small and cute, with his gray fur and black, beanlike eyes. Some people think rats are gross, but I don't think so at all. They just have a bad reputation!

"Hey, Mindy," Dad said suddenly. "Do you still fit into the hanbok that Mommy bought you last year? If you do, why don't you wear it to the parade since it's Lunar New Year? I know how much you love it."

A hanbok is a traditional Korean dress that people wear on holidays and special occasions. I wore my cute pink one last year, but I hadn't worn it ever since Mom died. Maybe it was time for me to bring it back out!

"That's a good idea, Appa!"

I ran up the stairs. I hoped that it'd still fit. My hanbok is really adorable, with pastel rainbow sleeves and a bright pink skirt. Mom and I spent a really long time in the hanbok store picking just the right one.

"Wait up!" Dad said. "Let me help you."

I rummaged through my closet until I found my hanbok. It was still wrapped in plastic so it wouldn't get dirty or wrinkled.

Dad helped me put it on. It was a little tighter and shorter than I remembered it being, but it still looked okay in my book!

"Hmm," Dad said. "Are you sure you're still comfortable in it? We'll have to get you a new one . . . somehow. I don't know if there are hanbok stores in Orlando, though."

"I can still wear it!" I said. "I don't care if it's a bit small."

Dad scratched his head. "If you're sure. I'm going to have to see if we can go up to Atlanta at some point later in the year so we can get you fitted for a new one."

I didn't want a new hanbok. The new one wouldn't be from Mom.

"This one is fine with me."

"Okay, I think it looks fine for now. Ready to go pick up Sally?"

"Yup!"

"All right." Dad smiled. "Let's go."

Chapter 5

When Sally got in the car, the first thing she did was tell me how pretty I looked in my hanbok.

"You look really nice!" she said. "Where did you get that dress?"

"It's a hanbok! And I got it in California," I said. "My mom bought it for me last year. It's a traditional dress that Korean people wear on special days like today."

"Cool!"

We headed straight for the parade in Orlando. While we were sitting in traffic, Sally took out a phone in a sky-blue case.

"Wow!" I said. "Is that your phone?"

"Yup! My mom bought it for me in case of emergencies, but I mainly just use it to play games. I'm not allowed to take it out at school, though. Wanna play?"

"Sure!"

Sally and I took turns playing a racing game that was super fun, even though Sally kept beating me by five hundred points.

"It's okay," said Sally. "You're really good for a beginner!"

When we were almost there, Sally put away her phone.

"I only have thirty percent battery left, so I'd better save it," she said.

We could hear the loud thumping of drums all the way from our car as we pulled into the parking lot. Everything else was drowned out by the loud chatter of the people outside.

"Wow, that sounds exciting!" said Sally.

Dad, Sally, and I got out of the car and walked toward the edge of the sidewalk, where we could get the best views of the parade.

Red Chinese lions danced with their mouths and eyes flapping open and closed, while long red and green dragons floated above everyone. People from many different parts of Asia came down the street wearing their traditional clothing. A lot of them smiled and waved at us as they passed, while others carried banners and flags.

I gave everyone a big smile as they walked by.

As I looked around at the other people watching the parade, I was glad that I wasn't the only one wearing traditional clothing. I didn't see anyone else wearing a hanbok, though!

"Hmm," Dad said. "Looks like there aren't any people representing Korea yet. The parade is still really interesting! Look over there at the taiko float, Mindy! Aren't those drums cool?"

Kids my age were walking down the street with taiko drums strapped across their chests. They were so good! The beat made me want to dance. Sally and I bounced up and down to the music.

It felt weird to see so many Asian people here. Even though there'd been a lot of Asian people back

27

in California, here in Florida I'd only seen a few. In the last couple of months, I'd become used to being the only Asian kid in my school.

"This is so cool!" Sally exclaimed. "I never knew there were this many different Asian cultures."

"This isn't half of it!" I grinned. "We haven't even seen the Korean stuff!"

We saw more dancers, musicians, and other performers. And we kept waiting for the Korean group to come.

"I'm sure there will be someone representing Korea at some point," Dad said.

Finally, after the last performers went by, it was pretty clear that we weren't going to see any Korean performers today.

Last year, at the Lunar New Year festival in California, there was a group of samulnori people playing Korean drums, flutes, and gongs. There was also a K-pop performance, where lots of pretty girls danced onstage with their supercool moves! Dad said the performers were college students who were in samulnori and K-pop clubs in school, and I remember hoping I could be one of them someday.

But no matter how much I waited, I didn't hear any Korean flutes or gongs this year. Nor did I see anyone dancing to K-pop. It made me kind of sad that there wasn't anyone Korean in the parade, even though seeing Lunar New Year traditions from other Asian countries was pretty neat.

Dad must have seen the frown on my face, because he said, "It's okay, Mindy. We can have our own Lunar New Year celebration back at home after the festival. I think we still have our yutnori board somewhere."

That made me feel a little better. Yutnori is a fun Korean board game that my parents and I used to play every Lunar New Year. Maybe I could teach Sally how to play!

Suddenly, Sally tugged at my sleeve.

"Look, Mindy! It's Pikachu!"

I whirled around and saw a huge Pikachu balloon pass by us in the parade.

"Wow!" I said. "It's really Pikachu!"

"Hmm, I'm not sure how Pokémon is related to Lunar New Year," Dad said, sounding really confused. "Maybe they just have it for the little kids."

"Let's go take a picture with it!" Sally said. She pulled out her phone from her pocket and started running into the crowd, toward the balloon.

I turned to Dad. "Can we go take a picture with Pikachu, Appa?"

"Um, sure. But wait—"

I didn't hear what else my dad said, because I started running when he said "sure." I was too excited! Dad was much faster than me, so I was sure he was close behind.

Sally ran toward Pikachu and I tried my best to catch up. It was kind of hard to run in my hanbok, and I had to hold my skirt up so I wouldn't trip on it.

The Pikachu was moving slowly enough that we could keep pace with it while taking pictures.

"You go first, Mindy!" Sally said. "I'll take lots of good pictures with you and Pikachu."

I smiled really big and put up the peace sign as Sally took pictures of me.

"Cute!" said Sally. She sounded like one of the moms who come to volunteer for our class. "My turn!"

Sally handed me her phone, and I took pictures of her. She looked so happy! I hoped I looked happy in my pics too.

"That was fun, Appa!" I said. "I think we can go home now. . . ."

I trailed off when I realized that Dad wasn't behind me like I thought he was.

"Wait," I said slowly. "Where's my dad?"

"I'm not sure," replied Sally. "Wasn't he right behind us?"

We looked around, but Dad was nowhere in sight.

"Maybe he's still walking by Pikachu!" Sally suggested.

But by then, Pikachu had gone way ahead of us. And we couldn't find the balloon again because there were so many people around us. And there was still no Dad.

We were lost!

31

Chapter 6

No matter how much I looked, I couldn't find Dad. Everyone was laughing and having fun, but I just wanted to cry. It was almost exactly like my nightmare, but instead of being alone, at least I had Sally with me.

I held it together, but barely. I didn't want Sally to see me cry and be scared too.

"Let's hold hands so we don't get split up," Sally said. "It'd be really bad if we lost each other, too."

"Good idea." I tightly grabbed Sally's hand. It made me feel better that no matter what happened, at least we were in this together. "It's okay," I said. "I'm sure we'll be able to find my dad soon."

"Let's try going back where we came from," Sally said. "Maybe he just got lost in the crowd somewhere along the way."

Sally and I started walking in the opposite direction of the parade. But no matter how much we walked, we couldn't find Dad, even when we reached the beginning of the parade.

"Maybe we can't find him because he's walking around looking for us, too." I tried my best to not sound scared, but my voice still quivered. I really hoped we wouldn't be lost forever.

"Maybe we can call him?" Sally suggested. "You know your dad's number, right? You can use my phone!"

I looked down at my feet. "No, I don't. I knew his California one, but he got a new phone after we moved here, and I haven't memorized that one yet."

"Okay, then, we can call my mom! She can get us, and then your dad can just catch up with us later. No problem."

Sally got out her phone. But instead of dialing her mom's number, she glanced at her screen and looked at me with wide eyes. "Oh no. We're doomed!" she wailed.

"Why?" I said. "What's wrong?"

"My phone ran out of battery. It won't turn on!"

"It's okay!" I said, trying to remain hopeful. "We can just ask to borrow someone's phone."

Sally shook her head. "I don't know my mom's number either. She's just speed-dial one. This is really bad." She sniffed. "I really want my mom."

"It's okay!" I said again, tightening my grasp on Sally's hand. "My dad is still looking for us. If we look for him, and he looks for us, we're bound to run into each other, right?"

We walked and walked and walked, but Dad was nowhere to be seen. Eventually, the parade ended, and everyone in the audience moved toward the end of the street, where people were performing on a big stage.

My stomach growled. I had no idea how long Sally and I had walked around to find Dad, but I was really hungry! And scared. What if we were lost here forever? Did Dad know we were still here? I wanted to find Dad. And I wanted food!

"I'm hungry," I said. "Do you want to get something to eat?"

"Sure, do you have money?" asked Sally.

"Oh . . . no, I don't." I was so worried about being lost that I totally forgot that you needed money to pay for food! Dad always bought food for the two of us, so I never carried money with me. My heart started beating really fast. Sally was right. We were doomed!

I was about to cry when Sally said, "It's okay! I have an emergency twenty-dollar bill in my phone case. You can pay me back later!"

Sally fished the money out of her case. She was a true hero!

"I don't know if twenty dollars is enough for both lunch and dinner, though," Sally said with a frown. "Maybe we can share something now and get something else later!"

She looked worried, and I bit my lip. I really hoped we could find Dad soon!

"Don't worry," I said, even though I was scared

too. "My dad would never leave us here. Maybe he just got hungry and stopped to eat something!"

Sally looked kind of doubtful, but she didn't say anything.

Together, we wandered over to the food stalls. There were so many options, but only a few were "within our budget." Sally explained that her mom says "within our budget" all the time during important business calls with her company. "It means that we have enough money for something!" she said excitedly. But then Sally's bottom lip began quivering. "What if I never see my mom again?"

I almost started crying too, when I heard Dad's voice.

"Mindy! Sally!"

I spun around. It was really Dad!

"Appa!" I yelled.

Dad ran to me and picked me up, squeezing me into a tight hug before snuggling his face against mine. His face was wet, like he'd been crying for a really long time. Seeing Dad cry finally made me cry too.

"It's okay, Dad," I said. "You found us! I'm safe."

"So, you were right about them being where the food is!" a lady said then.

I looked past Dad's shoulder to see a pretty Asian lady with short black hair. She looked happy to see me, even though I had no idea who she was.

"We were walking all over the place to find you . . . but then we got hungry," I said to Dad sheepishly.

He laughed and then smiled at both Sally and me. "Well, I'm glad we found you two in the end. You scared me!"

"Sorry we ran off," I apologized. "Being lost was really scary, so I promise I won't do that again."

"I'm sorry too," said Sally. "I was the one who ran after Pikachu first."

Dad patted both our shoulders. "It's okay, girls. I think we all learned a very important lesson today. Thanks for the apology, though."

"I tried to call you, but I forgot your number," I said.

39

"And my phone ran out of battery, so I couldn't call my mom," added Sally.

"Oh dear," Dad said. "Let's make sure you girls know all the important numbers when we get home. And next time, when you get lost, be sure to stay in one place so you're easier to find."

"Okay, Appa," I replied.

He then let go of me to gesture at the lady still standing behind him.

"Mindy, Sally, I want you to meet Julie. She's one of my coworkers, and I happened to run into her while searching for you girls. I kind of . . . panicked when I couldn't find you two, and she helped calm me down."

Julie waved him off. "It was nothing," she said. "Your dad looked like he needed help, so I helped! Anyone would have done it." She then waved at us with a big smile. "Hi, Mindy. Hi, Sally. It's so nice to meet both of you. I'm glad you two are safe."

I shook Julie's hand. "Pleased to make your acquaintance," I said, like they did in the old black-and-white movies I used to watch with Mom.

Dad coughed, and a mysterious look appeared on his face. "Well, Julie, if you don't have anything else to do, we'd love it if you'd join us for the rest of the festival."

"We would?" I asked.

Daddy shot me a nervous glance, like I'd said something I shouldn't have. He laughed, but instead of his usual booming laugh, his voice sounded weird and squeaky.

"Of course we would, Mindy! Don't be silly. Maybe we can all go grab lunch together? With the girls in very close proximity, of course."

Dad was acting very strange. I was about to ask him what was wrong when a man on the stage behind the food stalls announced, "Welcome to the Lunar New Year festival! We hope you enjoyed the parade. It's always so nice to see the traditions and festivities of the many different cultures we have here in Orlando. But don't leave yet! We have a lot of performances lined up for you here onstage today while you enjoy the delicious food. You're all in for a treat!"

"Quick," Dad said, gently pushing me toward a food-truck line. "Let's go get food now so we don't miss the show!"

"Okay," I said, narrowing my eyes. He wasn't off the hook yet!

Chapter 7

We ended up getting some yummy egg rolls and dumplings. Being lost definitely made me super hungry! But I still wanted to have our usual Korean New Year food too, so I mentioned it to Dad.

"Let's stop by the Korean supermarket on our way home and buy lots of our favorite food there!" he suggested.

It was the best idea I'd heard all day.

Carefully holding our paper plates of food, we walked around until we found enough seats for all four of us. It was really hard to find empty seats. By the time we sat down, our food had all cooled down.

"Wow," Dad said. "I can see why they had to move locations. This is a popular event!"

Compared to the Asian food in California, the food was just okay, especially since it was now cold. But the performances onstage were still pretty fun! There was a great group from Vietnam, who came out with parasols and danced. Then a couple of Chinese ladies danced with long, colorful ribbons. Every performance was so good!

Since there weren't any Korean floats or groups in the parade, I really hoped there would be someone performing onstage. I was just about to give up when I heard one of my favorite K-pop songs blasting from the speakers.

"This is it!" I yelled. "Finally, a Korean performance!"

I glanced at Sally to make sure she was paying attention to the stage. She was. I was so happy to show her something Korean, even though K-pop isn't *exactly* a New Year tradition!

After a few minutes, a group of five girls came

onto the stage. But there was something weird about the group.

Sally squinted her eyes. "Wait . . . is it just me, or . . . are none of the girls in that group Asian?"

"No, there's one Asian girl in the back," Julie said. "But you're right, Sally. Besides her, no one else is Asian."

"Hmm," Dad said. "I guess this is just a K-pop appreciation group. Maybe they're just trying to show how popular Korean music is?"

I didn't know how to feel about the group. They were really pretty and danced great! But I was still sad that during this entire day, we hadn't seen a single Korean person in the parade or festival.

I missed California.

Dad must have noticed that I was sad, because at the end of the last performance, he squeezed my shoulder and said, "Why don't we go back home and have our own super-awesome *Korean* New Year celebration?"

He turned to Julie and Sally. "And we'd be happy for you both to come, if you can? We can stop at the

Korean market first to pick up what we need."

Sally grinned. "Sure! I'm excited to try some yummy Korean food!"

I wanted to give Sally a big hug. I was so happy she could come over!

"Sounds like fun!" said Julie. "And yeah, if it's really okay with you, Brian, I'd be happy to join."

My jaw dropped. Julie was coming over to our house! Did this mean Julie and Dad were . . . *friends*? I got really excited. Finally, Dad was friends with one of his coworkers!

"Great!" Instead of saying "great" normally, Dad yelled so loudly that the lady in front of us turned to glare at us.

"Oops, sorry," said Dad. His face was getting a little red. He was acting so strange today!

Julie laughed and said, "Okay, well, text me your address and I'll meet you guys there after we go to the market."

While Dad was sending her our address, Sally tugged at my sleeve. She wiggled her eyebrows at me.

"Why are you acting so weird?" I whispered to Sally when Julie and Dad weren't looking.

"Mindy, I think your dad has a crush on Julie. And I think Julie likes him back!"

"But how?" I asked. "They barely know each other!"

Sally shrugged. "Adults are weird. Plus, they're coworkers, right? So they aren't *total* strangers!"

I didn't know how to feel about what Sally said. But I knew she was definitely onto something. I'd never seen Dad act that way around another person. He wasn't even that nervous around my mom!

Adults really confuse me sometimes.

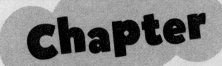

Chapter

8

On our way to the Korean supermarket, I asked Sally, "Hey, did you know that in Korea, we're nine years old?"

Sally wrinkled her nose. "What? How?"

"In Korea, you're already one year old when you're born. And then you age up whenever it's the New Year!"

"Whoa," she said. "That's pretty cool! Although I wouldn't want to be older than I am now."

I couldn't believe what she said. "What, really? How come?"

"The older you get, the closer you get to becoming a grown-up! And then you have to do scary things like pay bills and taxes! My mom told me that being an adult is the worst. And it looks bad too! She's always really busy and stressed."

"Well, I wouldn't say it's the worst," Dad said from the front. "You girls have a lot of fun things to look forward to. But it *can* be pretty challenging sometimes!"

Finally Dad found a parking spot. He barely had the car turned off when I flung open the door. I was ready to shop for all the food I'd missed out on today!

"Come on!" I said to Sally. "Let's go look at the snacks!"

"Mindy!" Dad said. "Can you please stay in the car until I get out? I already lost you and Sally once today. I don't want to do that again."

"Okay," I said, slumping down in the seat. I didn't want to wait, but I did anyway. I still felt bad for giving Dad a hard time earlier today.

In the end, we had to wait for Julie to park her car too. We all met at the front of the supermarket before we went in. There were so many people in the store that some of the lines were spilling out into the parking lot!

"Here's the game plan," Dad said. "We should all stick together, but just in case we get separated in the crowd, Sally should stick with me and Mindy should stick with Julie so each group has someone who knows what to look for. We need rice cakes, stir-fried glass noodles, and honey pastries, okay? And ingredients for jeon, Korean pancakes! Mindy, do you know what everything looks like?"

"Yup!"

"Okay, then, let's go!"

We went through the doors. Crowds of people filled the store, and loud, happy music was blasting from the speakers. Everyone was yelling and waving their hands in the air, trying to reach the products on sale. A lot of the food was already sold out!

"Quick!" I yelled. "Grab the rice cakes! And the honey pastries!"

"Excuse me! Excuse me!" Dad yelled as he pushed the cart around in the store. There were so many people, and Dad was too nice to push past them. Sometimes he even let other people push *him*!

"I have a better idea," said Julie, loud enough that all of us could hear. "How about Mindy and I go farther into the store to get everything we need in those sections? Brian, you can stay here with Sally and the cart."

"That's an excellent idea!" I said. "Now can we please go get the food?"

I didn't want any of the food to run out!

"Sure," Dad said. "I'll pick up a few things near the front of the store with Sally while you two do that. Let's meet at the cash register."

"Got it," said Julie.

Unlike Dad, Julie wasn't afraid to push past people. She wasn't mean and didn't hurt anybody, but she moved way faster and found everything we needed to find, plus a few more yummy things like dumplings and shrimp crackers. I liked Julie already!

By the time we were done, our cart was full of

snacks, rice cakes, sweet rice crackers, and stir-fried glass noodles.

It was finally starting to feel like a Korean New Year!

Chapter 9

When we got home, Dad got out our board and game pieces for yutnori, my favorite Korean game! It's a traditional racing game that people play on Lunar New Year. And before Mom got sick, my parents and I played it every year.

Last year, Mom, Dad, and I played against one another, but today, Dad said, "Since we have an even number of people, why don't we do teams? Sally and Mindy, you guys can be in one team while Julie and I can be in the other."

"But Dad, I want to be on a team with you!" I complained.

I was a little mad. Sally was my best friend.

But whenever we played games with our family or friends, Dad was always on my team. Why did Dad want to be on a team with Julie?

"But then who will I be on a team with?" Sally asked, sounding confused.

She had a point. Since Sally was my friend, I guess it made sense that she'd be my partner.

"Okay," I agreed. "Sally and I can be a team."

In the first few minutes, Dad and I taught Sally and Julie how to play. The game is pretty simple, since you just toss four sticks and move your piece on the board depending on how many sticks land faceup. If all of them land either faceup or facedown, it's super lucky and you can throw again!

"It's also really good if you land on one of the corners," I told Sally as the four of us sat down around the board. "Then you can cut across diagonally to the finish line!"

"Okay, got it," Sally said.

I didn't want Dad to win. First of all, I like to win! And second, I was still kind of mad at him for wanting to be on Julie's team.

Dad eyed the clock. "Usually, you're supposed to do two to four rounds, but I think we only have time for one round since we should start preparing for dinner soon. That sound good to everyone?"

Sally shrugged, and I said, "Yes!"

It was going to be a lightning round, all or nothing. I was so excited!

"Let's win for sure!" I told Sally, holding my hand up for a high five.

"Yes!" she said. "Let's!"

She gave me a high five.

I told Sally she could throw first. She threw the sticks, and they landed all faceup!

"Woo-hoo!" I cheered. "That was awesome. Throw again!"

This time the sticks landed with two of them faceup.

"Okay, so four from the first throw and two from the second," I said. "Move six places. That was a really good throw!"

Sally beamed and moved our piece forward

six times. We were doing so well already!

Dad rolled next. He got three sticks faceup.

"Oops," he said. "Sorry."

Julie smiled. "That's okay. It's only the first throw."

"Ha-ha!" I said as I picked up the sticks. "Now our team will win for sure!"

I threw the sticks.

They landed with only *one* stick faceup!

"Noooo!" I yelled. "This can't be!"

Dad chuckled. "That's too bad, Mindy. Maybe you'll throw better next time!"

Julie was next. She tossed the sticks and all of them landed facedown! All sticks facedown meant she could move *five* places, *and* she got to throw again! The second time, she threw the sticks and got two faceup. She moved her and Dad's piece seven times, and it ended up on one of the corners!

This was really bad. Now Dad and Julie had a direct path to the finish line. They were only six places away from winning!

"It's okay!" I said. "We can still win!"

I didn't want Sally to feel discouraged while she went.

She threw her sticks. This time she got three sticks faceup.

"Aw," she said. "Sorry for the bad throw."

"No, this is good!" I said. "Look where our game piece ended up!"

Thanks to Sally's throw, our game piece reached the same corner as Dad's and Julie's!

Game. On.

"No!" Dad yelled, like I had a couple of minutes ago. "You got us!"

"Wait," Sally said. "What's going on?"

"If you land on the same space as the enemy team, you can kick them out of the space and they have to go all the way back to the beginning!" I explained. "And then you can go again."

"Wow, that's so mean!" Sally said as she threw the sticks again. But she was smiling like I was. There's a reason why Sally and I are friends. "Sorry, Julie and Mr. Kim."

"That's quite all right, Sally," Dad said as he moved his piece back to the starting line. "That was a very lucky throw."

Sally's throw got us only two spaces this time, but it was way better than having to go back to the beginning. "Good job!" I said as she moved our piece.

It was Dad's turn, and this time, all his sticks landed facedown.

"Yes!" exclaimed Julie. "Way to go, Brian!"

Dad threw the sticks again. Three landed faceup. They had almost caught up to us already!

It was my turn to throw now. I was still really embarrassed that I got only one stick faceup the last time I went. But hopefully this time would be better.

"You can do it, Mindy!" Sally cheered. "Let's win this game!"

I stuck out the hand clutching the sticks in Sally's direction. "Let's do a lucky handshake!"

"Okay!" Sally's hand clasped mine so the sticks were sandwiched in between us. "Good luck!"

I then threw the sticks, and they all landed faceup! I threw again. Two were faceup. That was more than enough for us to win!

I moved our piece to the finish line and jumped up and down with Sally.

"YESSSSS!"

We won!

Chapter 10

After we cleaned up the game pieces, we went into the kitchen to prepare yummy food for our Lunar New Year feast.

"I just have to fry some kimchi, zucchini, and cod to make the jeon, and then we'll be all set!" Dad said.

Jeon are like pancakes, Korean-style. You mix all the ingredients into a batter and cook them in a pan like you do with American pancakes.

"Do you want me to help?" Julie asked. "I'm good with a knife and cutting board."

"I can help too!" I said. "What can I do, Appa?"

Dad nervously glanced back and forth between Julie and me.

"Well, Mindy, you can't help cut things or fry stuff in the pan," he said. "But you and Sally can be in charge of covering everything with flour after Julie's done chopping up all the ingredients! And then I can fry the jeon in the pan."

"Sounds good!"

We washed our hands, and then it was time for some food magic!

Just like she said, Julie was really good at cutting everything into thin slices. She was way better than Dad, who still accidentally hurts himself while cooking sometimes. He's the reason we have so many Band-Aids around the house, not me!

In almost no time at all, Julie had everything laid out neatly in a big plate, and Dad seasoned everything with some salt and pepper.

"Okay," said Dad after he took out the bag of flour. "Now what we're going to do is cover everything with flour. You have to make sure to get both sides of everything. I hope you don't mind getting your hands dirty, Sally, because this can get kind of messy!"

"I don't mind." Sally smiled. "It sounds like a lot of fun!"

Dad brought out the small pink aprons that I like to wear when I help Dad out in the kitchen.

"You girls can wear these. Sally, I don't want your mom to get mad at me because you have flour all over you."

Sally giggled. "Thanks, Mr. Kim."

Sally and I put on our aprons and started covering all the food with flour. I was afraid it might get boring, but with Sally by my side, it was actually fun! We laughed and joked around as we covered the zucchini, kimchi, and cod. We were done in no time, and Dad took out some eggs from the fridge and beat them in a bowl.

"Anything else I can do to help?" Julie asked.

Dad glanced around nervously again before saying, "You can help reheat the other things we got from the store while I make the jeon."

"Sure!"

Sally and I watched Dad as he took the flour-covered food and dipped it in egg before frying it in the pan. There was a cool sizzling sound whenever the food hit the pan, but after a while it got boring. So we helped Julie reheat the food in the microwave instead.

Soon the entire house was filled with the yummy smell of jeon, bulgogi, dumplings, and stir-fried glass noodles. It was a whole feast!

While we were eating, Julie, Dad, and I shared stories about the different things we did for Lunar New Year. Julie said that back home in New York, her family always gathered around and made dumplings. They also ate lots of fish and exchanged red envelopes that had money inside them.

Dad looked at me. "We don't do red envelopes like Chinese people do, but we *do* give New Year's money. That reminds me, Mindy. Do you want to do sebae after we finish eating?"

"What's sebae?" Sally asked.

"It's when I bow to Dad and wish him happy new year, and then he gives me some money!" I said. "Usually you bow to your grandparents, but my grandparents live far away from us, so I just bow to my dad instead. It's what people do for Lunar New Year in Korea."

"Wow!" said Sally. "How come we don't have traditions like that in America?"

"Beats me." I shrugged. "But if you bow to my dad, I'm sure he'll give you money too. Right, Dad?"

"Mindy!" Dad exclaimed.

Oops. I guess I shouldn't have said that!

Dad sighed. "Sebae isn't just about the money. Yes, a little pocket change is nice, but it's meant to be a way for your elders to bless you for the new year."

Julie laughed. "I can give some money too," she said. "Maybe I can give some to Sally, and you can give some to Mindy?"

"You don't have to," said Dad.

"Don't sweat it. It'd be my pleasure!" Julie said. "I just wish I had red envelopes!"

Dad got out comfy cushions and put them on the living room floor. He and Julie sat facing Sally and me.

"First, I want to make sure you two know why

we do sebae, because, like I said before, it's not just about getting money," said Dad, shooting me a look. "In Korea, respect for your elders is very important. So, in order to *earn* your money, you have to wish the adults a happy and healthy new year while you give them a deep bow. And the adults bless you, too. Sally, Mindy can show you how to bow."

"Yup!" I said. "I learned how at Korean school last year."

"Okay," said Sally. "Show me how!"

I went to stand right in front of Dad. He gave me a big smile.

"Well," I said. "First you put your hands clasped in front of your head like this, right hand over left." I lifted my hands so they were both at the level of my eyes. "Then slowly sit down, putting your left knee to the floor, and then the right."

Being careful to not trip on my dress, I knelt down onto the floor.

"And finally, bend forward so you're halfway to the floor before you stand up again."

I did my bow to show Sally.

"Wow," Sally said after I stood back up. "That looks hard."

"It's really easy!" I promised. "We can do it together!"

Step by step, I guided Sally into a proper jeol.

When we were done, I looked up to see that Dad was taking pictures of both Sally and me. He looked really proud, and Julie smiled at us too.

"You two were so great!" Dad said. "Happy Lunar New Year. Hope you both have a great rest of the school year! Study hard but don't forget to have fun, okay?"

"Okay!" we said.

After, Sally and I each got a twenty-dollar bill!

Now we were a bit richer!

Chapter 11

Soon it was time for Sally to go back home.

"Thanks for having me!" Sally said. "It was really fun! Well, except the getting lost part."

Dad frowned. "Right. I'm so sorry that happened, Sally."

"Don't worry, Mr. Kim," said Sally. "It was my fault anyway. Mindy and I were the ones who ran off after the Pikachu balloon! My mom will understand, I think. And I'll make sure to memorize her number!"

Her mom drove up to the front of our house, and Sally gave me a hug before she left.

"See you at school!" she said.

"Yeah, see you!"

After Sally was gone, it was time to say goodbye to Julie.

"Thank you so much for having me over," Julie said warmly. "I was bracing myself for spending this holiday alone, but in the end, I'm really glad that I didn't."

"We were glad to have you over as well," said Dad. "Mindy and I don't really know that many people in the area either, so it was great to see you."

Although I still didn't know how to feel about Julie, she *was* pretty nice, and we'd had a lot of fun together today. And I liked that she made Dad happy.

"Yeah," I said. "Don't be a stranger!"

Julie looked really happy, like Dad and I had just given her a puppy.

"See you at work, Brian," she said to my dad as we walked her out to her car. "And I'll see you around, Mindy?"

She gave me a big smile.

"Yup!" I grinned.

After Julie left, Dad and I went back into the house. What a day it had been! I wasn't sure if I could still love the holiday as much without Mom here to celebrate with us, but maybe I could still like it. And we could have new traditions and make new memories with our new friends.

Once I was back upstairs, I showered and put on my pink corgi pajamas. Even though the hanbok was pretty, it felt good to wear comfier clothes again.

Dad came to my room to tuck me into bed.

"Wow," he said. "We had a really busy day today."

"Yup," I said. "I hope the next Lunar New Year is more boring."

Dad laughed. "You and me both, kid."

He was about to leave when I said, "Appa?"

"Yes?"

"Do you like Julie?"

Dad's face turned strawberry red. "Why do you say that?"

"So, you *do* like her!" I said. "Sally said you did, and I guess she was right."

"Well," Dad said. "It's too early to tell. But she *is* very kind. We usually don't really interact with each other much at work, but today she helped me a lot when you girls went missing. Are you uncomfortable with the fact that I might like her, Mindy?"

I shrugged. I was a little sad because I missed Mom, but I knew Dad couldn't miss her and be sad forever. I don't think Mom would want that, either.

"I just hope she makes you happy."

Dad smiled, but his eyes were shiny, like he was about to cry.

"Aw, thanks, Mindy."

He gave me a little kiss on the forehead.

"But you have to tell me before you marry her, okay!" I yelled, jabbing a finger into Dad's chest. "And get my permission!"

Dad jumped in surprise. "Mindy! It's *way* too early for that. But sure, if that ever happens, with Julie or any other person, I will definitely let you know."

"Good," I said with a firm nod. "Good night, Appa."

"Good night, Mindy."

Dad turned off the light, and I moved Mr. Toe Beans back under my bed. I still had Mr. Shiba with me. One was enough for me tonight.

Even though it wasn't my birthday, I did feel older than I had before Lunar New Year. Today wasn't perfect, but it was definitely better than I thought it would be.

"Happy Lunar New Year, Mr. Shiba," I whispered to Mr. Shiba. "Congrats, you're now officially two years old."

Mr. Shiba, of course, didn't say anything. But he did look kind of happy.

I was happy too, as I closed my eyes. Even though I'd had a scary nightmare last night, I was sure I'd have a really fun dream tonight, filled with food, friends, and happy celebrations.

I was so excited to sleep! And I was even more excited for the Lunar New Year ahead.

Acknowledgments

When I first set out to plan this series, I knew right away that I wanted to write a book about the fun Korean traditions that my parents kept alive in our family despite the fact that we moved to the United States more than twenty years ago. Aside from the phone calls and infrequent visits back home, our traditions were the only way to keep connected to our roots. For that reason, I would like to thank my parents for never letting me feel any less Korean and doing their best to keep traditions alive in our family. 사랑해요.

I'd also like to thank my agent, Penny Moore, and my editor, Alyson Heller, who are always so enthusiastic about Mindy and her adventures.

Thank you also to Dung Ho, my illustrator, who never fails to draw such gorgeous and fun art for Mindy that Kid Me would have loved so much. You bring Mindy to life in ways I could have never imagined.

My friends, of course, were also vital to my writing process. Writing is often a lonely experience, and I'm so lucky to not have to go about this life alone. Thank you, as always, to Aneeqah Naeem, who is sitting across from me as I write this sentence. Our writing dates feed my soul. Thank you also to Katie Zhao, Amelie Zhao, Rey Noble, Faridah Abike-Iyimide, Sharon Choi, Francesca Flores, Annie Lee, Chelsea Chang, Shiyun Sun, Luke Chou, Anita Chen, Brianna Lei, Bernice Yau, Kaiti Liu, Angelica Tran, Oanh Le, Victor Hu, Eunji Lee, and all my other friends who make my life brighter every day.

I'm also so grateful for everyone who reached out and told me how excited they are to meet Mindy. Thank you especially to the teachers who have said they'll incorporate the Mindy Kim books, as well as other diverse literature, into their classrooms. You are changing so many lives, and we're all so lucky to have you.

Last but not least, thank you so much to you, reader! Thank you for joining Mindy as she goes on her adventures. I'm sure she's glad to have a friend like you by her side.

Don't miss Mindy's next adventure!

About the Author

Lyla Lee is the author of the Mindy Kim series as well as the upcoming YA novel *I'll Be the One*. Although she was born in a small town in South Korea, she's since then lived in various parts of the United States, including California, Florida, and Texas. Inspired by her English teacher, she started writing her own stories in fourth grade and finished her first novel at the age of fourteen. After working various jobs in Hollywood and studying psychology and cinematic arts at the University of Southern California, she now lives in Dallas, Texas. When she is not writing, she is teaching kids, petting cute dogs, and searching for the perfect bowl of shaved ice. You can visit her online at lylaleebooks.com.

Solve each problem with the smartest third-grade inventor!

Looking for another great book?
Find it
IN THE MIDDLE.

Fun, fantastic books for kids
in the in-be**TWEEN** age.

IntheMiddleBooks.com

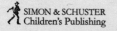